Treed by a Pride of Irate Lions

Treed by a Pride
of Irate Lions

by Nathan Zimelman
Illustrated by Toni Goffe

Little, Brown and Company
Boston · Toronto · London

First edition

Library of Congress Cataloging-in-Publication Data

Zimelman, Nathan.
Treed by a pride of irate lions / by Nathan Zimelman; illustrated
by Toni Goffe.
p.   cm.
Summary: Animals like Mother but not Father — so off he goes to
Africa where he hopes to find some loving animals.
ISBN 0-316-98802-2
[1. Fathers — Fiction.   2. Animals — Fiction.   3. Africa — Fiction.]
I. Goffe, Toni, ill.   II. Title.
PZ7.Z57Tr   1990   89-30344
[E] — dc19   CIP
                                                                    AC

10 9 8 7 6 5 4 3 2 1

WOR

Published simultaneously in Canada
by Little, Brown & Company (Canada) Limited

Printed in the United States of America

Dogs bit Father.

Cats bit Father.

Horses kicked Father.
Animals did not like Father.

"Why is it, Martha?" Father asked Mother. "Why is it dogs wiggle-waggle when you approach?

"Why is it cats twine about your legs?

"Why is it that horses, who cannot smile, do smile at the sight of you?"

Peter the Eighty-third, the family rabbit, butted Father and then jumped into Mother's arms and cuddled.

"It is a thing within people," said Mother. "Nothing can be done about it."

"Let go, Towser. That's a good boy," Father said as he tried to pry the family dog's teeth loose from his trouser leg.

"Bad boy, Towser," said Mother.

Towser wiggle-waggled but did not let go of Father.

"Something can be done about anything," Father continued. "I know I can make at least one animal love me. The question is, which one? As soon as I have milked the cow, I will turn my full attention to the problem."

"Be careful of the bull and gentle with the cow," said Mother.

"I am always careful of the bull," said Father. "I am aware that bulls do not like anyone."

"I wouldn't say that," said Mother, who had been known to take the bull for walks while wearing the green dress that went nicely with her blond hair.

"But I would, and I have. *And* I am always gentle with the cow," he said.

Father went off to milk the cow.

Several quiet moments passed while Mother waited.

"By now, John has gone by the bull safely," said Mother after a while.

"John has now entered the barn," she added.

"And now, John has placed the bucket beneath Bessie," she said with hope in her voice.

"Goop, goop, goop, goop," gurgled Baby.

Then there was a tremendous clang and a rolling clatter.

"Martha," yelled Father, "the cow has kicked over the bucket."

"Then turn it right side up, John, and begin again," called Mother.

"I cannot," answered Father. "The cow is standing on my two feet with all four of hers."

"Prepare a soothing basin of warm water, children," Mother said to us. "I will go and fetch your father."

Mother returned with Father, who was hobbling, his arm around her shoulder.

"Off with your shoes," said Mother, "and into the nice warm water."

"There is no time," said Father. "A great light has dawned."
Mother looked out of the window.
"John, that is the sun. It has been up ever so long."
"What I meant to say," said Father, "is that I have found out a why."
"Then that is what you should have said," said Mother. "What why?"
"Why animals do not like me," said Father.
"Why?" asked Mother.
"Because," said Father.
"John," said Mother, "I never understood 'because' when the children said it. I do not understand it now. Because what?"

"Because," said Father, "I have only given the tame, or domestic, animals a chance to like me, Martha. They are too refined for a man like me. I must go among wild animals. Martha, I must go to Africa. There I will find which is the animal for me. Expect letters."

"Goop," gurgled Baby.

"Oh, John, really," Mother laughed unbelievingly as Father passed through the doorway with Towser chewing on his trouser leg.

The door shut. The car started. It roared away. Then all was silence.

Mother stopped laughing.

"Children," Mother said, "I believe your father has really gone to Africa. How extraordinary. We will await his first letter to inform us which of the many wild animals of Africa likes him."

"Boop," burbled Baby.

Several weeks passed and then the mailman drove up to the mailbox.
"Look, children, a letter from your father.

"'Pursued by a herd of angry elephants,'" read Mother. "'I stop briefly to drop you a note. As for the animal, it is not elephants.

"'P.S. Towser sends his regards.'"

"I can hardly wait for Father's next letter," said Mother. "We must count the days."

"Goop, goop-goop, goop," gurgled Baby.

We counted ten days before the mailman drove up again to the mailbox. "Look, children, a letter from your father.

"'Mail delayed,'" read Mother. "'Treed by a pride of irate lions. It is not lions.

"'P.S. Towser sends his regards.'

"Children," said Mother, "today we shall start to pray for your father."

"Boop, boop, boop," burbled Baby.

We prayed every day until the postman returned.

"Ah, just in time," said Mother. "We were almost out of prayers. Look, children, here is a letter from your father, a very damp letter from your father."

Mother peeled the envelope as a banana is peeled. She took out the letter and held it up to her spectacles. She peered at it.

"The words seem to have run together," said Mother. "However, if I spell out the words a message will be sure to appear.

"'I-t i-s n-o-t c-r-o-c-o-d-i-l-e-s,'" Mother spelled out.
"'P-S T-o-w-s-e-r s-e-n-d-s h-i-s r-e-g-a-r-d-s.'

"If we sing, children," said Mother, "time will just scoot by."

"Gooo, gooo, goo, gooo," gurgled Baby.

"La, la, la, la," sang Mother.

We were all quite hoarse by the time the mailman finally drove up to the mailbox.

"Look, children, another letter from your father.

"'Excuse pencil,'" read Mother. "'An irritable giraffe has swallowed my pen. It is not giraffes.

"'P.S. Towser sends his regards.'"

Mother put the letter away and sighed. "Perhaps games will pass the time," she said.

We had played hide-and-seek ten times and charades twenty-two when Mother cried, "Look, children, a letter from your father, a crinkled letter from your father. Fetch the steam iron so that I may iron out the envelope, iron out the letter, and see what your father says.

"'It is not boa constrictors,'" read Mother.
"'P.S. Towser sends his regards.'

"I hope that your father does not meet any rhinoceroses,"
said Mother. "It is so difficult to read around holes."
"Goo, goo, goo, goop," gurgled Baby.
Mother sighed and began to look worried.
Just then, the front door slammed.

"Hello, dear family," said Father, coming through the doorway with Towser fixed firmly to his trouser leg.

"Welcome back, dear," said Mother. "Did a great light suddenly dawn?"

"Yes, Martha," said Father. "Just as an exasperated rhinoceros prepared to charge, I realized that it did not matter if animals did not like me. It is enough that I am loved by my family. So I have returned to you and the children. I am now at peace."

Father kissed Mother.
Father bent to kiss Baby.
And Baby bit him.